Mizpah

Afra Job

Published by Afra Job, 2023.

MIZPAH

First edition. July 3, 2023.

Copyright © 2023 Afra Job.

ISBN: 979-8223933144

Written by Afra Job.

Table of Contents

To the people who stayed and cherished

To the people who looked down on me

....

To the 3 who always stood beside

To the 2 who always pacified

To the 1 who always loved

To all those beautiful chapters which I would love to re-read,

To all those seasons and places I dwelled,

To all those amazing humans I've met,

To all my loving FamRiends.

CHAPTER ONE

Only love serves as the cornerstone of the universe. What more could one ask for when humanity triumphs over rivalry?

Triveni is the home of the innovative academy, where the future kings from all over the world come to take practical lessons. Young princes from different provinces are enrolled in the academy to learn about archery, politics, arts, sports, and other topics. These young princes are being trained in many different ways so that when they return to their native land, they will be able to rule with wisdom and benefit the people there. Two Asian kings who favoured peace among nearby countries founded the academy.

Fortunately, the mission was a huge success, and over the years, princes who spoke different languages gathered together at the age of twelve and stayed there until they turned twenty-two. The institution was a global family rather than just an academy.

When the brotherhood was in charge of their souls, differences in languages, cultures, or traditions were not obstacles.

Among the batchmates were two princes who had a special bond with one another. One was a Korean prince, and the other was an Indian prince. Despite their many differences, they were bound together by love. They also picked up on each other's languages. They shared an unbreakable bond as they grew up together.

The academy had a tradition of allowing the students to take a four-week vacation every year. They could return to and stay in their home for these four-weeks. They both paid a visit to the other prince's place. Their family greeted them with open arms, which started a cordial relationship between the two cultures.

Ultimately, love transcends language.

As time moved on, those princes matured into talented and intelligent young men who were all poised to succeed their fathers as rulers of their respective provinces. It's now time for them to part ways. It was the saddest time of their lives.

How challenging is it to leave the family we built through love? -Friends.

Their fathers, who were then in charge of their respective provinces, led them on an escorted journey back to their home country. The two friends find it difficult to leave the place. From the academy of Triveni, Prince Yashwant and Prince Minseon bid each other farewell and vowed to keep their friendship going. They kept in touch by exchanging gifts, messages, and invitations to their unique ceremonies. For the rest of the world, how these two princes maintained their friendship was beyond belief. A few more years passed, and now they were twenty-eight. Both princes were now willing to get married.

The decision of who to marry was left up to them.

CHAPTER TWO

Prince Yashwant chose Princess Nanda from the neighbouring province. She was her parents' only child, and her wisdom was unparalleled. She will be the next ruler of her land following her parents' reign. One day, Prince Yashwant travelled to the kingdom of Ajayapuri to attend an annual gathering of princes from other provinces to demonstrate their abilities in art, sports, and academics. He, as the prince of Praudapuri, represented his abilities.

His talent left the audience in awe. The representative from Ananyapuri then entered the stage to perform. Everyone was shocked to see that it was a woman. A female state representative was uncommon to see. She was Ananyapuri's princess. Prince Yaswant was impressed by her slick movements during the sword duel. She was also sagacious. Once she'd finished her act, he was the first to clap for her. The presence of a woman with such courage in public, however, did not please all of the people who had gathered there.

"Did the king of Ananyapuri lack men, and is that the reason he would send a woman?" asked one of the princes.

Another person responded, "I heard the king only had a daughter, and is she going to rule her province after her father?"

Princess Nanda stood silent. She had the option of responding to them, but she didn't want to risk damaging her kingdom's reputation. And besides, there is no use in talking with fools.

Prince Yashwant unexpectedly stood up for her. "To everyone here, with due respect, I wanted to address this matter. Why is it wrong for a woman to act so bravely in a public place? It would be better to respect her talent than to make her feel embarrassed. She made all of her moves with great precision, at least in my opinion as someone who studied martial arts for many years. Even those so-called "experienced men" often make mistakes, but she never missed a move. I would encourage everyone who has gathered here to congratulate her for the efforts she has made. Let us pass on the legacy of equality. We must continue the tradition of honouring our mothers, sisters, and daughters."

The whole crowd was awakened by his wise words. The princes apologised to Princess Nanda right away after realising their error. She and the other Princes received honours from the king of Ajayapuri during the closing ceremony. She went to Prince Yashwant to express her gratitude. She was happy to see a Prince with such a great vision. After all, the only person who could have offered such words of support was her father, the king of Ananyapuri. She recalled how the king's lack of a male heir caused the ministers to express concern. The king, however, was confident that his daughter would take over as ruler of the state when he passed away.

Even some of his close relatives suggested that he adopt their sons and make the next heir. She was raised by her loving father, who refused to marry another woman, after losing her mother when she was just two years old.

He said, "How could half of my soul be filled with another when my soul completely relies on my queen forever?" He loved his late queen very much, and no one could ever replace her. Princess Nanda grew up witnessing her father's admiration for her deceased mother. She often pondered whether she would ever find a man who would love her unconditionally, just like her father did. Other states came to the princess with marriage proposals. The king believed that she should have complete freedom to select the partner she would spend the rest of her life with. Princess Nanda thinks she has finally met her match at this point.

She looked for Prince Yashwant, who was getting ready to return to his home with his friends. She sent one of her assistants to ask him if he could meet her near the river bank, which was on the outskirts of Ajayapuri. He went to meet her after accepting the invitation. When he arrived, he saw her standing there in her royal garb. He was mesmerised by her hair's graceful dance as the wind passed through it. She turned around to greet him when she felt his presence. There was nobody near them. It was a private meeting.

"Greetings Prince Yashwant. I'm glad that you accepted my invitation."

"Greetings Princess Nanda. Why should I decline the invitation of a bold lady?" Prince Yashwant replied. "It is an absolute honour for me that you asked me to meet."

She replied, "I... I wanted to thank you for supporting me when I was hesitant to speak. I was aware that if I said anything, they would come up with false accusations. But, Prince, I should sincerely thank you for taking my side. After my father, it was only you who spoke for me. Thank you very much."

"It shouldn't be brought up," said Prince Yaswant in response. "Never in my life have I witnessed a woman with such bravery. I'm interested in learning from you all of those unique techniques. I hope that one day you will be remembered as the woman who broke down barriers and became a role model for others."

Princess Nanda was overjoyed when he complimented her. She could tell how sincere his words were. His eyes lit up as he spoke.

"Thank you Prince, for your kind words," she replied. "Please accept this gift as a token of my appreciation." She then handed him the bouquet of red lotuses she was holding.

"My goodness, these look pretty," he said as he took them. "Where did you get these?"

"This morning, we went for a walk with the princess of Ajayapuri," she explained. "We noticed a group of children struggling to collect these lotuses from the pond. We helped them and took a few for ourselves."

"That's very kind of you," he said. "Do these red lotuses have any particular significance?"

"Well, red lotuses symbolise care and affection," she explained. "You were the only person who cared about me at the time, so I gave them to you."

"It was very considerate of you to choose these," he said. "And I accept them."

They continued to talk for a while, and now they need to resume their journey. In hopes of reuniting soon, they said goodbye.

The trees that witnessed their meeting now rustled in the wind. It was as if nature herself didn't want them to part ways. They started walking in opposite directions.

Red Lotus is for love.

Even though they were aware of the symbolism, they preferred not to mention it. He held the flowers close to his heart. It was like an indirect confession. The prince and princess arrived safely in their respective states and told their families about their romantic interests. Surprisingly, the two kings were close friends when they were students at the academy. However, their relationship broke down as a result of some unexpected circumstances. Both kings could rekindle their friendship through this proposal. It was formally announced that Prince Yaswant and Princess Nanda were getting married.

CHAPTER THREE

Back in Korea, arrangements were made for Minseon to wed Hye-Jung, a princess from the neighbouring state. She had a compassionate nature. Her kindness caused him to fall in love with her. They first met each other when she was visiting his place. There was an elderly woman who developed a strange illness and lost her sight. She was an immigrant who had to leave her homeland due to poverty.

Their cruel ruler frequently subjected the citizens of his realm to torture. She lived alone in a tent built near the border of both the states of Minseon and Hye-Jung. Her husband and son died while they were crossing the river on a rainy day. The river took them away. The princess once saw this blind woman fumbling with her clothes after they got tangled in a thorny bush. She was on her way to meet her sister, who had travelled to Minseon's state to attend a carnival where musicians and dancers from around the world would display their art forms. The princess exited the chariot and assisted her.

After thanking her, the elderly woman inquired about her. The princess understood the possibility of the elderly woman becoming frightened if she revealed her true identity. Instead, she presented herself as a regular woman from the neighbourhood. They talked for a while. The old lady was happy to have her company. She asked her whether she could visit her daily. The princess agreed. Her sister was waiting for her arrival in town while this was happening. It was getting late. She grew anxious.

The ruler of the state was informed of this situation. Prince Minseon, his son, was given the mission of finding her. It would be a great shame if the visitors to his province were attacked or left with a bad experience while they were there. He went to the border after spending many hours searching. He noticed the royal chariot there, which was parked alongside the river with a few soldiers nearby. When he approached them, they respectfully bowed. When he asked where the princess was, they replied that she was inside the tent with the old lady. He received a full account from them. The prince wondered how a Princess could spend her time with an old lady while her sister was anxiously searching for her. He entered the tent and saw the princess feeding the blind old woman some hot soup.

"Greetings Princess Hye-Jung."

When she turned around, all she saw was a young man—likely a prince—looking bewildered and dressed in a regal robe.

The sudden arrival of a visitor at the elderly woman's home startled her. "Who's there? A princess?" she asked confusedly.

"Yes Grandma, she is Princess Hye-Jung," Prince Minseon responded. "Her sister was worried because she hadn't shown up in town to meet her, so I went looking for her."

The old woman asked, "My child, are you a princess? Why did you lie then?"

After giving Prince Minseon a serious look, Princess Hye-Jung responded. "Pardon me, Grandma. I thought you might get intimidated if I said I am a princess."

The old woman said, "It's alright my dear. But I'm grateful that a kind person like you spared your time to spend it with a simple, undeserving woman like me who has nothing to give in return. May God reward you for your kindness."

They hugged each other, and both the prince and princess left for the town. Prince made arrangements to ensure the elderly woman had a better quality of life.

They reached the place, and Prince Minseon narrated the whole incident to the king and her sister. She had done a good deed, and the ruler was moved by it. He said, "My child, you are a precious soul." The queen embraced her and blessed her. She caught the attention of Prince Minseon because of her personality. He thought to himself- 'This is what royalty means: a kind heart to serve people no matter what circumstances they are in. A woman with a pure heart and no ego would be willing to give her own life to serve her people. She would make an excellent monarch'.

After receiving many compliments and gifts from the king and queen, Princess Hye-Jung and her sister returned to their province.

Their father was informed of this. He considered forming a relationship with the state after being pleased to hear that. Hye-Jung's sister was already married to another prince, so now Hye-Jung is left to get married. The province accepted his proposal after receiving it, and they were delighted to have her as their daughter-in-law. Due to his existing romantic interest in her, Minseon accepted the proposal. Hye-Jung, however, insisted on speaking with Prince first before making a choice. They were scheduled for a private meeting.

In their palace garden, she waited for him. When Prince Minseon arrived, he presented her with a bouquet of *red lilies*; in return, she gave him a bouquet of *dark pink azaleas*. They greeted one another before sitting down to speak. Princess Hye-Jung started the conversation.

"I assume that you're aware of the marriage proposal. I have no objection to this, but I wanted to say something about myself. Though I was born into the royal family, I am not fascinated by the riches that I hold. I just wanted to live a simple life and serve my people. If you are fine with that, we can proceed otherwise–"

Prince Minseon listened to her with patience. "Princess Hye-Jung, with all due respect, let me apologise for my hurried intervention," he said, speaking out of the blue. "Since I have already met the world's most compassionate person, I am not considering anyone else. I could marry a princess from a rich state, one with many riches and treasures. But I've never met a woman with a mind as sophisticated as yours. I do not doubt that you will make the ideal queen for me when I become king. Together, we will be there for each other."

Princess Hye-Jung blushed upon hearing his words. They eventually agreed to the marriage proposal. Both provinces were happy with the news.

Prince Yaswant's and Prince Minseon's marriages took place a week apart. Prince Yaswant and Princess Nanda were the first couple to wed. As special guests, Prince Minseon and Princess Hye-Jung attended their wedding. The four of them formed a strong friendship group. Both princesses held one another in high regard and exchanged tales of their first encounters with their beloveds. They sent them well wishes and a bevvy of priceless gifts that they had brought from the land of the morning calm. With great joy and satisfaction in their hearts, they returned to Korea.

The day of Princess Hye-Jung and Prince Minseon's wedding approached quickly. The special guests were the newlywed Princess Nanda and Prince Yaswant. The two friends attended each other's weddings and rejoiced that they had started families. The prince and princess from India were overjoyed to experience Korean hospitality. The ceremonies went well, and both couples said their goodbyes and agreed to visit regularly.

CHAPTER FOUR

A few more months went by. They were both leading peaceful lives. They were anticipating the arrival of their first child. The Indian royal family and the Korean royal family exchanged gifts for their heirs. It made them happy to see that their families were growing. They hoped to pass down the legacy of their friendship to their children as well. One morning, it was announced that Princess Nanda had given birth to a healthy baby boy. This news reached Prince Minseon and Princess Hye-Jung. They were really happy. A few days had passed since the baby boy was born. Meanwhile, in Prince Minseon's palace, Princess Hye-Jung was in a critical situation. The royal physicians warned him that she would have complications during childbirth. Prince Minseon was taken aback when he heard this. He couldn't watch the love of his life suffer such a fate. For the state, doctors from other nations and even Prince Yaswant's state were urgently gathered.

The Prince did everything he could think of to save her life. She struggled with labour on the due date, and after many hours of agony, she gave birth to a healthy baby boy. Unfortunately, Princess Hye-Jung did not survive. She died as a result of excessive bleeding. Prince Minseon stood motionless. He sobbed while holding the baby. As he ran to see his love, the king and queen took the baby from his grasp.

There she lies, cold, with no smile on her face and only the dried trace of tears on her cheeks.

He approached her bed and embraced her cold body, asking, "Where is the warmth you held? Where has your pleasant smile gone? Love, please open your eyes. How could you leave me so soon when you wanted to grow old with me and hold my hand until the end of the world? Remember the promise we made that you would be my queen when I become the king? Don't leave me in this darkness alone..." He cried out loud and fainted.

Death could only separate the mortal body, but never the immortal soul!

His trusted friend, Prince Yaswant, came to visit him and consoled him. Even Princess Nanda arrived there along with her baby. She was shocked to see her sister lying lifeless. She recalled the pleasant times they had spent together and how they had promised to raise their kids to be best friends just like them. Due to the loss of her best friend, she was unable to hold back her tears. Prince Yaswant regarded Hye-Jung as a sister. He assured her that he would be there for her whenever she required a brother's assistance. He also lamented the loss of his cherished sister. Princess Nanda went to hold Prince Minseon's newborn child. She was reminded of Hye-Jung by the baby's face. The infant's face was peaceful and innocent. The king and queen were at a loss for words and helpless to console their beloved son.

She was their ideal and devoted daughter-in-law. Princess Hye-Jung's funeral was held with the utmost respect. The Indian couple stayed there for a week more and continued to strengthen Prince Minseon They then returned to their homeland. Princess Hye-Jung's parents asked if they could take the baby with them to raise him.

"My son is the most precious gift I have received from my beloved," Prince Minseon said in response. "He is a part of her. How could I leave him when it would be through him that my beloved would live?" They didn't respond with anything. They were confident that the child would be safe with his father because he adores him deeply. He ceased speaking after the passing of his beloved. State-related issues no longer piqued his interest. As they grew older, the king and queen were no longer able to manage state affairs to their fullest potential. They considered Minseon's coronation as the next ruler. But he rejected it. The king and queen sat down to talk with Minseon.

"Son, we understand how painful it is to lose your beloved one," the king said. "However, because you are descended from royalty and will one day rule, you cannot always remain isolated from society. Please do not forget about your duties towards our people."

The queen added, "If the baby is your concern, we could arrange a caretaker for him."

"No, no, nobody would ever care for my son the way I do," Prince said abruptly. "I cannot do that."

The king said, "My son, try to understand. As the child grows, he will require a mother's love. Now look at us; we are getting old and weak. How long could we possibly handle everything? And also, the kingdom needs a queen anyway."

"Stop it already!" yelled Minseon. "Queen, you say! She was and will always be my queen. Nobody could ever replace her. How could you say that to me?"

Suddenly the baby boy cried, and he went near the cradle and took him in his arms.

His mother replied, "It's fine if you don't want a queen, but you can never deny that he needed a mother to love and care for him."

They both exited his room after telling him this. They wanted a good life for the baby and their son. They wanted to see the happy face of Minseon again.

"I am sorry son; I could provide you with all the happiness you desire but never the love of a mother," he said to his son. "Nobody will ever be able to replace your mother. But someday, if you yearn for a mother's love, I might be helpless. I will therefore agree to this only for you."

He kissed the newborn baby boy on the forehead.

CHAPTER FIVE

One year has passed. The baby boys grew older. The loss of his loved one was still hurting Minseon. It had already been two years. His parents are now bedridden. He found it challenging to manage both the state's issues and look after his son, Taeho, at the same time. The idea of getting married was put forth again by his parents. He struggled with this matter for a long time before deciding to wed a princess. She was a widow and had a son who was a few months older than Taeho. Minseon agreed to the marriage because he believed Lim Maya would take good care of his son since she was already a mother. She was married to the king of another Korean province. But he passed away suddenly. People suspect that the enemies might've poisoned him. His death left Lim Maya a widow. There were not many festivities for Lim Maya and Minseon's nuptials.

Only a few people, including Prince Yaswant, were invited. Due to her three-month pregnancy, Princess Nanda was unable to attend the wedding, but she still sent the newlyweds gifts and wishes. The wedding went well. Yaswant was reminded of Minseon and Hye-Jung's wedding and how he helped with all of the arrangements. Reminiscing brought a tear to his eye. As soon as the function was over, Prince Yaswant went to greet the couples. He gave them presents. In addition, he gave gold chains to Taeho and Lim Maya's son, Lim Jae Wook. He took the babies in his hands and blessed them. After that, he returned to India, hoping that his best friend would now be happy again with his life.

Their lives were happy for a while. But soon his parents died due to illness and old age. Minseon's sorrow was heightened by these sudden events. He lost his beloved first, and now his parents. He believed that he might have been cursed by God because he would not have suffered successive tragedies if he were not. He thought of living for his children, including Lim Maya's son. Both of them were very dear to him. After his parents passed away, he was crowned the king of the state. Because Minseon was not mentally ready to make Lim Maya his queen, she was given the title of the prince's mother instead of the queen. But she was given access to every other power.

When Minseon learned of the second child born to Prince Yaswant and Princess Nanda, he travelled to India with his family. It was a baby girl. They were given a warm welcome when they arrived at the palace. Tejas and Tejaswini were the names of the couple's elder son and newborn daughter, respectively. They recalled their past while playing with the children. They hope that once they grow up, they too will be sent to the academy, just like them.

They had fun together, which helped them unwind after a string of unanticipated events. The young Korean princes were given traditional Indian clothing by Princess Nanda, and Lim Maya was given some exquisite jewellery. The newborn baby girl received an enormous number of gifts from Minseon as well.

"I feel like she could become my daughter-in-law one day," he said while holding the infant and chuckling.

Prince Yaswant agreed that it would be a wonderful idea so that they could continue the bond as a literal family.

"Let's wait until they both grow up and if they're willing, then we'll plan on this," Princess Nanda said. It served as a sort of mood-lifting joke.

"Is it about Taeho or Lim Jae Wook?" Lim Maya asked curiously.

"Oh! we were just making jokes", Princess Nanda said. "How could we predict their future? Moreover, they are babies, right? They are free to decide who they want to spend the rest of their lives with. However, an alliance between each other's families would not be a bad idea".

King and his family returned to Korea after staying there for a week. Several more years went by. Prince Yaswant's parents passed away in those years because they got older and weaker. King Minseon arrived to support his best friend and to take part in the coronation ritual. Right now, they are each ruling their respective kingdoms.

A generation has passed, leaving memories of innocence, love, and mishaps for the future.

Life is a journey of ups and downs. Sometimes a human life ends before reaching its goal, just like a leaf that falls before it withers. And that is life—the most spectacular story with the most unexpected twists.

CHAPTER SIX

When the young princes were old enough, they were supposed to be sent to the academy to receive their training. Prince Tejas, Prince Taeho, and Lim Jae Wook grew up to be pretty young boys. They are now prepared to enrol in the academy. Lim Jae Wook declared he wouldn't be attending the academy because he found the idea of leaving his home repulsive. The king could not help but concur with him. He feared that if he disagreed with him, maybe he would starve himself, fall sick, and lose him too. He sent Taeho to the academy. When they reached Triveni, King Yaswant was already there with his son, Prince Tejas. Upon seeing one another, the two boys gave each other hugs. The fathers admired them and were ecstatic to learn that even their sons would uphold their goodwill.

King Minseon gave King Yaswant an explanation of the situation after he inquired about Lim Jae Wook. King Yaswant could see how considerate he was towards his stepson. Tejaswini was sent to spend time with her grandfather, the king of Ananyapuri, who was living alone. They sent her there because they didn't want him to be lonely. She would visit her family regularly and spend her childhood years with her grandfather, as he explained in response to Minseon's inquiry about her. The kings left the place after enrolling their sons in the academy.

Like their fathers, the two princes spent their next ten years at the academy. They were both wise and courageous as they grew older. They mutually taught each other's languages and even travelled to each other's places. They spent their time with Lim Jae Wook, who was a few months older than them when they went to the province. He was like an elder brother to both of them. They even shared their academy lessons with him so that he could also benefit from their knowledge. He seemed more like a composed individual who enjoyed the arts and music. He entertained his brothers by performing on various musical instruments. He might grow up to be a fantastic singer. He didn't want to learn archery, but his mother insisted that he do so. He was a simple human being and was not fascinated by the riches of royalty. He frequently composed music for his stepfather.

No, not stepfather; he was never like that. The two of them never treated each other that way. A few more years have passed. Now the princes were close to completing their course. Only a few more months left. The academy was informed of some sad news one day.

The state's ruler, King Minseon died of sudden heart failure.

Prince Taeho was shaken by this news. He couldn't believe his ears. His father, whom he admired the most, has left him. How could this be so early? He was waiting to return to his kingdom and spend time with his father.

Death is the unexpected villain.

King Yaswant and other members of the royal family travelled to Korea with Prince Taeho. As soon as they arrived, memories from the past began to trouble them. There were both joyful and sorrowful moments for King Yaswant. How he met his lifelong friend Minseon, how he got married, the day Taeho was born, how Princess Hye-Jung passed away, and so forth. The warm welcomes of his father whenever he visited during their vacation were Taeho's memories of his childhood home, where he lived until he was twelve years old. However, everything has changed now.

There lies; a father, a brother, a best friend, and a king -motionless.

When he saw his best friend dead, King Yaswant could no longer contain his grief and cried aloud. When Taeho fell to his knees, Prince

Tejas grabbed hold of him and held him close. He sobbed as he hugged Prince Tejas.

A hug, kiss, smile, or cry could sometimes fill the gaps left by words.

CHAPTER SEVEN

The funeral ceremonies were held with royal honours, and he was cremated near his beloved. A week had passed since the terrible incident. After his father's passing, Prince Taeho had no desire to go back to the academy. However, he was compelled to finish school by his brother and King Yaswant.

King Yaswant advised him, "My dear son, you must make your father proud by being brave and shrewd like him. For me, you are like Tejas. As if I were your own father, pay attention to what I have to say. You must do it for yourself."

Prince Taeho couldn't disagree with a man he regarded as a father figure. Both princes went back to the academy. Whenever Prince Taeho experienced emotional lows, Prince Tejas reassured him of his strong support. Like a shoulder to cry on, he was always there for him.

Months went by. Their time at the academy was completed. Despite the disturbing events of recent months, they continued at a steady pace, thanks to each other's support. The time had come for them to return to their respective provinces. To escort Prince Tejas, King Yaswant arrived at the academy. From the state, Prince's brother came to take him back.

King Yaswant accompanied him, as he didn't want him to feel the absence of a father's affection. Grand celebrations, planned by his stepbrother, were held to celebrate his return.

The princes and Lim Maya were summoned to an urgent meeting by the court ministers the following day. King Yaswant was invited to join them by the two princes. The ministers all concurred so that they could receive a knowledgeable recommendation from the king. The sudden agenda that was presented dealt with the new king's coronation. Many months have already passed since the land went without a ruler. The state needed a ruler because Lim Maya is only entitled to the role of the prince's mother. Traditionally, the firstborn son of the ruler is the next heir. Even though Lim Jae Wook was Minseon's stepson, he considered Lim Jae Wook his own. Prince Lim turned down the offer to become the next ruler when the ministers and Lim Maya suggested it, believing it to be improper.

"Even though I'm not the late king's blood relative," he said to the council, "I feel tremendous honour to be regarded as his eldest son. To be the sovereign, however, is not my goal. It calls for a great deal of maturity and responsibility. I think I'm incapable of completing tasks that do not interest me. If I become ruler, I won't be in a position to properly perform my obligations. *A thing done half-heartedly is more dangerous than doing nothing.* I hope that my brother, Taeho, will be the ideal heir to the state. I think he deserves to be in this position." Hearing the words of the prince, there was a brief moment of silence.

"My dear brother, I do not think I would be able to do it," Prince responded. "I'm not certain about my capacity to lead an entire land."

In response, Prince Lim said, "I believe in you; you will be the best king, and I will always be your brother."

When the council saw the brotherhood, they were in awe.

In his remark, King Yaswant said, "My children, this unity is what makes you the best siblings. Your father would have been happy for your companionship. Ministers, what do you say? Should Taeho be crowned the new ruler of the state? What is your opinion on this, your highness, Lim Maya?".

Lim Maya said, "If that is their wish, who are we to go against? Taeho shall be anointed as the next ruler of the province."

The decision was accepted by all of the ministers. However, the prince must gain a basic understanding of how the political system in his state works before being crowned. As he had assisted their father in those matters, Prince Lim decided to assist him as well.

CHAPTER EIGHT

It was decided that a period of six months would be given to Prince Taeho to study the royal administration so that he would also be able to get along with his people. During that period, everyone helped him towards the successful accomplishment of his task. The people of the state were happy because soon they would get a ruler who would rule them just like the former ruler, the late King Minseon.

King Yaswant ensured that he would be there for him in the place of his father. Taeho couldn't ask for more. He thought that his father, being the king, had all the riches, but among the best was the friendship he had with King Yaswant. Not only had he been a good friend to his father, but he was also his greatest comfort. He was thankful for his father's friendship with King Yaswant.

Three months have already passed. Prince Taeho was progressing in his task. The court ministers already knew that he would make a great king. Lim Jae Wook was immensely happy to see his brother receiving praise from everywhere. King Yaswant, Rani Nanda, and Prince Tejas visited the state. They were like a family. Prince Lim Jae Wook, Prince Taeho, and Prince Tejas went for a ride to the nearby woods. They had a fun time together. It was like having a moment of relaxation in the middle of a hectic routine. They got off their horses and sat down under a tree. They talked for hours.

Then, Prince Taeho spoke, "Brother, I wanted to ask you something; you seem happy for the past few days. Is there any special reason for your happiness?". Prince Lim Jae Wook smiled shyly.

"I think he is in love. Only love could make him shy. Tell us, who is she? When will we be able to see our sister?" Prince Tejas asked teasingly.

Lim Jae Wook replied, "Well, you guessed it right. I'm in love with a woman. She is the daughter of an artist who drew the royal portrait.

She is also a good artist. Once, when I visited their place, I saw her draw a portrait of a man holding a harp, but he was faceless. She was shocked to see me all of a sudden. When I asked her why the picture didn't have a face, she replied that she would complete the face of the man once she met the love of her life. It felt like a prayer. I was moved by her words. How well she defines! Eventually, we came to know each other and our interests and fell in love".

The two listeners were able to recognise the love he had for her; it was evident. Even though Prince Taeho was shocked by the sudden reveal, he was happy that his brother had finally found love. He would now have someone to share his joys and sorrows with.

He asked, "Did you talk with your mother about this?"

Prince Lim Jae Wook replied, "No, not yet. But I am afraid of what would happen if she disagrees by saying that she is not from a royal family. But whatever may come, I will live for my love".

"Don't worry, brother, you'll succeed. Ultimately, only love wins. Besides, the future king himself would help you. Isn't it Taeho?". asked Prince Tejas.

"Yes brother, no matter what, we will always be there for you," Prince Taeho assured.

The three of them went back to the palace. King Yaswant and his family went back to India, and they would come back for the coronation of Taeho.

Time went by. There were only a few more weeks until the coronation day of the new king. Prince Taeho asked his brother to invite his lover to the official ceremony, and he would introduce them as a couple to the court soon after he was anointed as the king so that nobody could object to a king's statement. Prince Lim Jae Wook became so happy. He took his horse and headed off to his lover's house to bring her with him.

A day passed, two days passed, and still, he didn't return. Prince Taeho became anxious. He took a few of his men and went to search for him. He sensed something bad but didn't want to believe it. No information was received, and they went back to the palace. Only a few more days remain until the coronation. While they were waiting for the Prince's arrival, a messenger rushed to the court. He was heavily sweating and panting. Fear was visible in his eyes.

He spoke in between his hard breaths, "Prince... Prin... prince... he... a woman... river... Prince Lim Jae Wook and a woman were found dead near the south valley."

Prince Taeho fell to his knees after hearing the news. He wasn't able to cry or speak. He became numb. He rushed outside and saw men carrying his brother's body inside the court. They put it down. Taeho ran towards it and removed the cloth that covered his brother's face. He gently touched his face. He wasn't able to cry; not a single drop of tear left his eyes. He embraced his brother's body and stayed like that for some time. Some of the men came to take him away, but he held his brother very close, not wanting to leave him. He was like a small kid who hides behind his mother.

After some time, he was forcefully taken from there. He sat down. He didn't care about the dos and don'ts; it was his brother lying cold and dead. He saw their mother mourning the death of her son. He was such a kind person who was loved by all. King Yaswant received the news of Prince Lim Jae Wook's death on his way to attend the coronation and became restless. He wanted to reach Prince Taeho, as he knew that he needed them the most.

They reached the palace. Prince Tejas ran to find Prince Taeho. As soon as they both saw each other, Prince Taeho cried out loud and hugged him tightly. It was like he was waiting for his arrival to pour out. Prince Tejas couldn't accept the fact that Lim Jae Wook was no more. King Yaswant came to the young princes. He thought how unlucky he was to see the demise of his best friend then and his son now. He was also concerned about the state of Prince Taeho, who lost his family. He wondered how he would tackle all these unfortunate events. He prayed that Prince Taeho would be strong enough to face them all.

Prince Taeho learned about the woman who was found dead near his brother. It was his lover. She would have been his sister if she were alive. He wanted to see her, and that was the reason he sent his brother to bring her, but not like this. He would have been able to see his brother living a happy life. But everything is ruined now. The prince demanded that the woman be buried with his brother. He was the only one who knew about their love. Everyone stood amazed when he revealed his brother's love. He did this because it was the only thing he could do to unite them.

If not in life, then in death, let it be.

The rituals were all done, and Prince Lim Jae Wook was buried with royal honours.

He slept peacefully on the earth, singing songs that could no longer be heard by anyone but his beloved.

The strings of the earth

The ministers approached King Yaswant and requested that he talk with Prince Taeho about the coronation ceremony. They did it because the prince told them to cancel all the plans. But if the absence of a king continued for longer, their province's administration would be in danger. King Yaswant was convinced about the situation, and he went to talk with Prince Taeho.

At first, he rejected all of his requests, as he was now completely broken. But at King Yaswant's insistence, he agreed to resume the ceremony. King Yaswant stated that this would be the greatest tribute he could ever offer to his dearly departed.

The coronation took place elegantly. Everybody was happy except for the fact that they had lost their dear prince. Now King Taeho is the new ruler of the state. It was both a sad and a happy moment. Happy that the prince is now the king and sad that they've lost their family.

CHAPTER NINE

Life must go on.

King Yaswant, along with his queen and son, stayed there for a few more days. They comforted King Taeho to overcome the current situation. Now they were preparing to go back. A group of people had also accompanied King Yaswant from India, who showed an interest in establishing trade with Korea and exploring their culture. These people voluntarily came forward without any compulsion when King Yaswant set out a notice asking for interested people who wished to do the same. He thought that it would help them understand the culture and grow in harmony with each other. The group included traders, artists, scholars, and ordinary workers. They were happy to visit Korea, but now the scene has changed into a sad one because of the death of Prince Lim Jae Wook.

King Yaswant thought that these people and the natives of Korea would create a good bond with each other. When King Taeho came to know about this, he was happy that even in the middle of immense sadness, his fatherlike figure, King Yaswant, showed concern for the betterment. He felt like a part of them living here would ensure him that King Yaswant was only one call away to help him.

He agreed, and the group stayed there. It was hard for King Yaswant and Rani Nanda to say goodbye to King Taeho, whom they considered their son. Prince Tejas was happy and helpless at the same time. He was happy that the prince became king but was sad about his return. They went back after a while.

The state is now ruled by King Taeho.

The very first thing he wanted to find out was about the suspicious deaths of his brother and his lover. He knew that his brother's lover lived in the eastern part of their state, but how did they end up in the South Valley? It was evident that they weren't attacked by any wild animals. As per the diagnosis made by the royal physician, both of them were stabbed to death. They might have been attacked by the robbers, who took away their ornaments and sword. But, as a part of the coronation ceremony preparations, soldiers were sent to every border spot to ensure that there were no invaders. Then how could this happen? He ordered his chief commander to investigate this. He wanted to know who killed his brother. He also made sure that his lover's family was taken care of. That is all he can do now. He visited her family and ensured that he would bring justice to them. They could trust him like a son.

A few more days passed. Everything is getting back to normal except for the sad memories. Lim Maya decided to spend the next few months in her native land. King Taeho thought that she needed a change from this place. The king wished to meet the people who came from India. They were invited to the palace. They offered him the presents they carried from India.

Aditi devo bhava

CHAPTER TEN

King Taeho was glad to see them. The group included both men and women. Each of them was skilled in one way or another. He was pleased to see their willingness to establish trade between both provinces. The king made sure that they had no trouble living here.

At that moment, one of the ministers spoke, "Your majesty, I have heard that Indian cuisine is diverse and tasty; it would be great if they could introduce us to some of them."

It seemed like a good idea. He recalled travelling to India with Prince Tejas and relishing the cuisine prepared by Rani Nanda herself.

He endorsed the notion. A few of them were permitted to remain at the palace. Additionally, they showed their readiness to participate in landscaping and other beautification projects. A fusion of the two cultures would be incredible. A group of twelve people stayed back. This group included scholars, poets, artists, singers, dancers, cooks, gardeners, and so on.

Several more weeks went by. The palace's appearance began to change. It was possible to see an incredible fusion of Indian and Korean styles. It improved the aesthetics. The king preferred to eat meals that included Indian cuisine. Some of the greatest crafts were produced through the collaboration of artists from the two provinces. The king was astounded by how well both groups got along. This should be the quality every human being should exhibit to avoid conflict among nations and sustain peace on Earth.

One day, as he was walking towards the palace's library, he noticed a young girl—probably a year or two younger than him—taking care of a kitten in the garden. It had injuries, so perhaps other animals had attacked it. She was actually speaking to the kitten. King Taeho thought it was amusing and decided to listen to her conversation. She has got to be an Indian. She spoke their language.

He could understand what she was saying to the kitten because he was fluent in the language, thanks to Prince Tejas from the academy.

She was scolding the kitten while displaying concern for it.

"Why did you go there? I am sure I have told you that there could be big cats and dogs there. See you, you poor thing. It's fine, and next time, don't you dare go there."

She treated its wounds and took it in her arms. She kissed the cat. The king observed everything with a slight smile on his face.

The woman suddenly turned around, only to find the king leaning on the pillar with his hand-held cross. She immediately bowed with respect and greeted him, "Greetings, your majesty."

"Good day, young lady. Are you a member of the Indian group that arrived?" He inquired.

"Yes, your majesty. I belong to the group," she agreed.

"Well, it was kind of you to treat that kitten. What is your name? And what kind of activity do you engage in inside the palace?" he asked.

"Your majesty, my name is Padma; I am a performer and a writer. I also teach children," she replied.

"That's great to hear. Being talented in many ways is indeed a blessing. I hope you will join the palace's official group soon. It would be a great asset," he insisted.

"Thank you, your majesty. It would be my honour."

Just then, a messenger came and informed him that Mother Lim Maya had returned from her place. King Taeho went to receive her. Seeing her again made him happy. She had recently experienced a lot, and he was aware of that. Happiness returned to the kingdom under the new king's rule. In order to see the province's accomplishments and developments, people from the neighbouring kingdoms would travel there. A few more months went by. King Yaswant received the good tidings of King Taeho's wise leadership. He became proud to see his greatness. He pictured how pleased his deceased friend would have been to witness his son's success.

A few more months passed.

CHAPTER ELEVEN

It was a happy time of the year. The neighbouring state's ruler, Jun Woo, and Prince Min Jae visited the state. Back then, Min Seon and Jun Woo were close friends. King Taeho and Prince Min Jae were fellow students at the academy. The guests were greeted at the palace. On the occasion of their arrival, festivities were arranged. King Jun Woo recognised similarities between the personalities of King Taeho and his deceased friend. Like his father, he is very kind and generous. They gifted him many presents, which they brought all the way along. Cultural programmes were held for entertainment.

To everyone's surprise, the Indian group and the locals from the state gave a special performance. It was a visual treat. Everyone was enthralled to see how well the two cultures coexisted to produce such a wonderful treat. Padma led the dance, and everyone applauded once the performance was over. She once again left King Taeho in awe of her talent. How elegant and graceful, he thought. He became absorbed in her performance.

Prince Min Jae noticed his state of mind and asked him in a voice that only both of them could hear, "How graceful she is; are you perhaps in love with her, dear king?"

Taeho came back to his senses when he asked that. He responded while stuttering, "Oh, it is nothing like that. It's just that I haven't seen such professionalism before."

Prince Min Jae was sure that his friend had already fallen in love with her. The way his eyes sparkled, the small smile that passed his face when she played solo. He hoped that after all those unfortunate things, his friend would find happiness.

Happiness and honour filled the heart of King Jun Woo. He appreciated the performers and gave them special gifts.

After that, they went to eat. Tasty cuisine was awaiting them. During their meal, King Jun Woo remembered a past event and told them.

He said, "Your father was the bravest man whom I have ever seen. I will always be grateful to him. My son would not be here today if it were not for him."

The princes were around five years old when that incident occurred. The king of a nearby province used to take advantage of his subjects and plunder their wealth for his opulent lifestyle. He tortured people and made their lives unbearable. Some of them started to migrate to the state. When King Jun Woo learned about this, he offered help to the migrants and also sent a warning to the cruel king. He would be detained by the Union of Provinces if he persisted in his behaviour.

The cruel king became enraged, which led him to kidnap King Jun Woo's son while they were visiting the country shrine. King Jun Woo was helpless because one wrong move would result in the death of his son. The ruthless king had the young prince in captivity. He was kept in a cave close to the dense forest of the borders. Minseon, the king of the state, was informed of this. He went to support his pal. He was still reeling from the loss of his beloved at the time. He, therefore, had a deep understanding of the suffering caused by the loss of loved ones. It was something he did not want to happen to his friend. In order to save Jun Woo's son, Minseon secretly embarked on a mission with a small group of his trusted men. The tyrannical king was finally subdued and put in prison after a protracted battle. The little prince was kept alive. Minseon risked his life to save him. After many years, they learned that the cruel king had broken out of the prison and fled and that no further evidence had been discovered.

The unexpected recollection of the incident did, in fact, extol Minseon's bravery. King Taeho felt very proud that he had such a great legacy. The guests left the palace after two days. They said their goodbyes.

CHAPTER TWELVE

However, a strange thing occurred a short while after they left.

The king used to spend some alone time in a quiet area of the palace's garden. He gave the order that no one should enter for the next few hours so that he could sit by himself. He asked for food and drink to be brought over there. He took a seat on the bench and thought back on the lovely memories. He juggled feelings of joy and sadness.

His thoughts were interrupted when a voice called him. He turned around to see Padma holding a tray filled with food and water. He was amazed to see her.

"Greetings, your majesty," she said as she placed the tray and started to serve them. He asked out of curiosity, "Why are you doing this? Isn't there anybody else to do them? I don't remember you saying that you help with the service."

She responded, "Your majesty, I apologise if I violated. I thought of helping my friend. She wasn't feeling well, and I insisted on doing her task."

Taeho replied, "No, there's no need to seek an apology. I was just asking. So, then, how is your life here? I know you people had the best life at Uncle Yaswant's place. We are delighted to accommodate such a talented group of people. I hope you enjoy living here."

"Your majesty, there is no doubt that we had the best life back in India. We wanted to explore new cultures, and that brought us here. And honestly, we are happy here. The natives are already like our family members," she replied.

"Good to hear that. And speaking of your performance the other day, it was full of grace. I wonder how all the people from India are this talented."

"Thank you your majesty for your words of appreciation. But I would like to add to that statement if it doesn't offend you. The performance was a mix of both cultures. The success came only because of unity, and I am deeply thankful to my group members who stayed united. It all happened because of our minds working together."

"I agree to that. And I hope for greater innovation in the future," the king replied.

They continued to talk for a while. She had a strong command of many topics, so he was delighted to hear her speak. She is unquestionably gifted in many different areas.

They were having a pleasant conversation when a man with a face mask emerged from the bushes. He was holding a knife. He was going for the king. They carried on speaking without noticing the sudden intruder. He moved silently towards them. But at that moment, Padma saw him and pushed the king to the ground so he would not be stabbed. Unfortunately, while attempting to save the king, Padma was hurt. The king was not carrying any weapons. He stood up and managed to defeat him. Hearing loud cries, two soldiers instantly arrived on the scene. They took the attacker away with them. King Taeho assisted Padma in reaching the royal physician. Though she only had a minor injury in her right arm, the king commanded that she be treated without fail. He ensured that she was well. Then he left to find out more about the attacker. Unfortunately, he managed to beat down the soldiers and escape. They could not see his face because he was still wearing his mask, which he resisted them trying to remove. The king gave orders to have him apprehended as soon as possible.

The chief commander approached him and showed him the knife that the enemy had used for the attack. Taking them in his hands, the king gave them a thorough inspection. He became numb for a second.

The royal emblem of Jun Woo's state...

He couldn't believe his eyes. He thought he might be hallucinating. But no, it was not. The knife had an impression of Jun Woo's state emblem. The chief commander confirmed that it belonged to his state.

But why?

Why would they attack the king? They bid farewell on a good note the other day. He thought perhaps there was a problem somewhere. The chief commander doubted that maybe the attacker used that knife, so they would suspect that it was an attack from their state. It might be a deliberate one. King Taeho strongly believed that it might not be an attack from them. It was someone else in disguise.

But who and for what?

The unknown enemy or the known?

Everyone became more cautious as a result of the sudden attack, and the king was particularly determined to identify the mysterious foe.

He went to visit Padma to ensure that she was treated well. But to his surprise, she had already left the infirmary soon after she got the first aid. When he inquired about it, the physician said that she told him that it was just a small injury and that she was grateful for the care she received. She didn't want to bother them. The king personally went to meet her. He saw her writing something. She was taken aback when she met him. She stood up and greeted him.

"Greetings your majesty."

He had genuine concern in his eyes. She could actually feel it. He approached her, took her right arm in his hands, and looked at the wound on her arm.

"Are you sure that you are fine? Why did you leave early?"

"Your majesty, it was only a scar, and I got treated. I am glad I could shield you from the assault. And I apologise for pushing you down all of a sudden. I couldn't think of anything else other than to save you."

He sensed how courageous she was.

"As the king, I must ensure the safety of my people, even if it would cost my own life. You put your life in danger to save me, and I am incredibly grateful for that. Padma, you have my eternal gratitude."

"I feel honoured, your majesty. As a fellow human being, the king's life is just as valuable as that of his subjects. A rightful king like you should live longer for the welfare of the people. No matter who it was, I still would have acted the same."

This reminded him of his mother, Hye-Jung. She was a woman who helped others selflessly. It was the main factor that made his father fall in love with his mother. The members of Padma's house were amazed to see the king himself at their place. They welcomed him warmly and gave him their undivided love and respect. He enjoyed himself and returned to his palace. He became relaxed, and it lightened his mood.

The king's mother, Lim Maya, invited Padma to the court to thank her for saving her stepson's life. She was also invited to join Lim Maya for the entire day. When he observed that they were both having a good time with one another, King Taeho was delighted. At the end of the day, Padma returned to her house.

CHAPTER THIRTEEN

Everything remained the same for the next few months. Only peace and happiness. Even so, the king was driven by a burning desire to identify his foe. But no information was found. King Taeho was certain that a formidable foe was latent and would one day emerge.

But why? What was the reason?

Time moved on.

Eight months had passed since the coronation of the king. Prince Tejas made an unexpected trip to Taeho's palace one day. King Taeho was overjoyed to finally see his friend again. Many things have changed since they last met. The friends had a lot to talk about. He was like a family member. The ministers went to speak with them. They all treated him as if he were their own. Both King Taeho and Prince Tejas went out for a ride. They went to the same place where they met before Prince Lim Jae Wook's death. This place brought back a lot of memories. It was like the three brothers' secret place where they would meet to spend time together. But one of them is no longer alive.

Prince Tejas was able to understand the pain, and he tried to cheer up Taeho. They talked about the sudden attack of the enemy, state affairs, family, and the future. Prince Tejas talked about a princess whom he happened to see when he went to meet his grandfather at Ananyapuri. He described how he had already started to fall in love with her and that he might eventually get married to her. Taeho was surprised by his confession. He was aware that not just any woman would appeal to his friend, but rather someone special. He recalled Rani Nanda, the mother of Prince Tejas, talking about how he used to pass up other provinces' princesses who longed to capture his attention. He merely remarked, "They do not seem to interest me." Taeho was delighted that Prince Tejas had, at last, found his soul mate.

He asked about his sister when he mentioned his grandfather. He knew that she was staying with him for a long time.

"Oh yes, Tejaswini, she has gotten older and is still with our grandfather", Prince Tejas said in response.

Taeho recalled their childhood. How much fun they had playing whenever they visited one another.

Everything's past; look forward to the future.

They went back to the palace. The group that came from India visited their Prince Tejas, at the court. He was happy to see them living peacefully. The king had sent gifts to give them. Prince Tejas gave them away. A young woman from the group suddenly caught the prince's attention. Other women had long hair, whereas she had short hair that probably reached the length of her neck. That surprised him because he had never seen a woman with such short hair. He was not offended by that, but he found it something different and interesting. Prince Tejas spoke to each one of them personally.

When he reached to talk to that short-haired girl, he asked out of curiosity, "Greetings, young woman. If you won't feel offended, let me ask you why you have short hair. I find it unique and good. Is it some sort of tradition that you follow?"

The woman replied, "Greetings, Prince Tejas. In order to keep a promise I made to my grandfather, I cut my hair short. But sorry, I cannot explain anything further".

"No, it doesn't matter; I just asked, and I respect your opinion. God bless you."

King Taeho was standing next to Prince Tejas, listening to all of their conversations. Only then did he also realise that woman's hair. He could not believe that, despite being around Padma for months, he had never noticed that she had shorter hair than the other women, who all had long hair. He had always been more impressed by her talent and character than her looks. While Prince continued to talk with the other members, Taeho was thinking about how beautiful Padma is. There is no doubt that she is wise and talented. She is also very beautiful. She is tall, with brown skin, and her eyes are filled with life. She always smelled like tulsi—fresh and herbal. She epitomises intelligence and beauty.

It is not about being fat or thin or black or white; it is all about being healthy, neat, and clean.

Prince Tejas stayed a few days in the palace and went back to India.

The prince brought some saplings from India, and King Taeho insisted Padma help him plant them. Every time those two friends got together, they had a very regular habit of exchanging saplings.

This time, it included gulmohar, banyan, and numerous other medicinal plants. King Taeho was slowly falling in love with her. What is there not to like about her: her willingness to work, her love of nature, her skill with words, her vision, and her diligence? Deep down, he felt that there was something different about her from the rest of the women he had met. He thought maybe their souls were connected. Even Padma felt different when she was around him. He thought that the fact that he was a king might intimidate her from engaging freely with him. But none of those titles would ever restrict a person from falling in love.

People love the souls, not the titles. If not, it ain't love, because love can never be faked. If it is not love, then it is hate. Love is a true emotion.

They get to know each other well. King Taeho was expressing his love for Padma, whereas he felt she was restricting herself. He didn't know the exact reason.

As the days passed, Padma distanced herself from Taeho. He couldn't tolerate her absence. He already had many losses. He would fight for his love. He decided to confront her. He wanted to know why she was separating herself from him. He sent a messenger to invite Padma to meet the king.

Padma arrived at the palace. She was guided to the royal library, where the king was waiting for her. She went inside the library and saw King Taeho reading the scrolls. She went near him and greeted him.

"Greeting your majesty."

King Taeho looked at her as if he wanted an explanation from her about the sudden isolation.

"Greetings Padma, may I know why you didn't show up for the past few days? Is there something bothering you? May I offer you my help if you require any?"

"No, no, your majesty, nothing is bothering me. I am fine-"

"No, you are not; I could already tell it from the way you speak. Tell me about it. I am here to listen to you."

"Well, your majesty, I think it is not a good thing for me to spend the majority of my time here in the palace. I was assigned to assist my friends here. I feel like I am running away from my responsibility by spending time here with you. It wouldn't have been a problem if I were a member of the court. But I don't think it is appropriate".

"Who told you this? With due respect, let me ask you, my lady, what made you think that way? I am the king, and I do not feel anything strange about it."

"Your majesty, soon you might be receiving marriage proposals from other provinces, and you would have to choose your queen then, so I do not intend to create any misunderstanding in between."

"Yes, you are right; I choose my queen. And I don't need to choose a princess to be my queen. I would marry the woman I love; maybe she could be a princess or not. And I think it is the right time to tell you that-"

"Sorry to interrupt you, your majesty, but I know where it's headed. I know what you are going to say. Please don't. You deserve somebody else, not me."

"See, you already knew what I was trying to say even before I spoke. Is it a crime to love a woman who could read my mind—a woman who could hear the words unspoken? I do not believe in class or rank. It is only love that matters."

"Your majesty, you are putting me in a difficult situation."

"No, I am not; it is not like I am compelling you to love me. I know you love me too. But something is taking you back further. Tell me about it, my lady; let us get through this."

"I am sorry, your majesty. I am only an immigrant here, and maybe someday I will go back to my homeland. I have my responsibilities as a daughter and as a sister."

"Then let's be a family, so that I can also help you with it."

"Your Majesty, I also heard that your marriage to our king's daughter was decided upon a long time ago."

"Padma, that was a long time ago, and I never made a commitment to wed her. I would only marry the woman I love."

She was consistently rejecting Taeho's assurances of his support and love. He loved her and was afraid of losing her, just like his beloved.

"I cannot take it any longer; I am returning to my homeland", Padma abruptly declared, startling the king.

Taeho felt sorry for making her angry. She left the place in a rush when he started to apologise. Maybe she will get more annoyed. He doesn't want her to think of him as a troublemaker. Perhaps she needs time and space to think.

But...

What if she goes back? Will I have another chance to meet her? I can not force her, though. He became anxious as a lot of questions began to surface in his mind. He remained in the library for some time. He was unable to move or think. He just sat there. Negative thoughts started to rule over his head. He closed his eyes and sat down, thinking of them.

CHAPTER FOURTEEN

After some time, he left the area. A guard came and conveyed the message that the royal court members, along with his mother, were waiting for him to discuss the upcoming spring festival. It's been a while since they celebrated the spring festival grandly. This was the first spring festival after Taeho became king. The ministers wanted to celebrate it in a very lively manner. If this festival would make his subjects happy, then King Taeho believed that it was worth celebrating.

Even his stepmother said that the festival this year should be special. The king agreed to the same and commanded that he delegate the tasks to make them the best. Professionals were assigned to handle particular tasks. Everyone began to participate in it. People were actively engaging in various activities and contributing their best to make the festive season even better. Fifteen days were left to begin the festival. King Taeho ensured that Padma was assigned certain tasks in which she could excel. Although there is a distance between them right now, they both appreciate each other from afar.

Though far, yet near.

He thought that maybe after the festival he would talk to her again and make her speak to him openly. The ceremony was approaching quickly. The whole province glowed differently during the spring season. Everywhere there are happy faces, happy songs, good food, and so on. King Yaswant and his family had been invited by King Taeho to participate in the festival. He loved to celebrate with them. The royal family arrived at the palace two days before the ceremony, and Padma was in charge of taking care of them. He did this on purpose to introduce her to them and see how they would react to his choice of her as his queen.

Padma completed her tasks perfectly, as usual. Taeho always believed in her. The spring festival usually starts with the family members visiting the shrine, which is located near the outskirts of the countryside. The journey takes two hours from the palace. There is a tradition that only close members of the royal family, along with a few guards and servicemen, should accompany the king to the place.

It is believed that the deity in the shrine, whose name is unknown, enjoys peace and dislikes the idea of a large crowd. Many years ago, the province was ruled by foreign forces that looted and destroyed the land. They also destroyed the forest, which was the abode of the god. The god became furious, attacked the invaders, and restated peace on the land. From then on, only the king's family and their servants were allowed to enter the shrine. King Taeho, Lim Maya, King Yaswant, Rani Nanda, Prince Tejas, the chief commander of the army, guards, and a group of other people went to visit the shrine.

But why would the Indian royal family join them? Aren't they foreigners to the land?

Prince Tejas inquired about it with King Taeho.

"Brother, we do not belong to the family, and I am aware of the tradition that nobody else other than the royal family is allowed to enter the shrine. What if something bad could happen if we disobeyed them?"

To this, King Taeho replied, "Brother, I understand your concern. I am not doing anything against the norms; I am taking my family with me to visit the shrine." He glanced at Padma. "Aren't you like my brother, and aren't your parents like my own father and mother? You are my family. So what's wrong with it? Now can you deny that?"

Prince Tejas couldn't disagree with that. He always loved Taeho as his brother. When Taeho said those words, he was amazed and thankful.

A family created by love.

Padma was also included in the group. Taeho wanted her to join him to visit the deity. He wanted to introduce her to the god who saves the land. He also wanted to seek blessings from God for his love life and to thank him for all the blessings he had. They reached the shrine, and the ceremony began. The worship did not begin until after dusk. They paid offerings and prayed for the prosperity of their land.

After the prayers, the spring festival season was officially inaugurated.

They were getting ready to go back to the palace. However, all of a sudden, they began to hear horses neighing and marching noises. The army was alerted by the sudden invasion of enemies. They pulled out their swords and got ready to fight. They saw a group of men with weapons in their hands marching towards them. The king ordered the guests and other people to move to a safer place. Prince Tejas, Rani Nanda, and King Yaswant also took up their swords to fight.

The battle began. They battled one another. They were furious because of the sudden attack and fought with their enemies. The cruel king, who had long since escaped from prison, was the leader of the opposing gang. He came to take revenge on King Minseon for punishing him. King Minseon, however, is no longer alive, so he decided to exact revenge on his son, King Taeho. King Yaswant identified the enemies and shouted out while defeating one of them.

"Son, he is the cruel king who escaped a long time ago."

The evil king laughed hysterically when he heard this and then said, "Well, my dear old friend, you still remember me. Yes, I'm the one you were looking for. King Taeho, how could I ever forget your father humiliating me? but he left earlier, before my arrival. That is fine. Now, I could kill his son." He laughed just like a maniac. Taeho was abruptly captured by a few of his men. He had his sword taken from him. Everyone else was fighting with each other.

"May you soon be with your father." He took his sword and ran towards Taeho. It was impossible for him to escape from their grasp, despite his best efforts. He closed his eyes and thought this might be his end.

The end of Taeho

CHAPTER FIFTEEN

But suddenly he heard a loud cry. He opened his eyes and saw a person who was covering the face, and started to fight with the cruel king. Prince Tejas came to rescue Taeho and was able to arrest all of them after freeing him. The unknown warrior continuously fought with the cruel king. Finally, the cruel king was defeated and chained. He became totally weak. Taeho was eager to know who the mysterious warrior was. The mysterious warrior, however, sprinted away into the shadows before he could approach. He was sure that it must be a skilled man with excellent swordsmanship. He wished to identify that individual and express his gratitude for saving his life.

But now the priority is to punish the cruel king they've captured. All of them returned to the palace. King Taeho made sure that none of his people lost their lives. Thankfully, a few of them were only left with minor injuries. There were no casualties. First aid was provided as soon as they reached the palace. As soon as they learned about the unexpected attack, the entire town gathered around the court.

The cruel king was brought to the main courtyard in chains along with his fellow culprits. As soon as he was brought in, people recognised him.

In front of everyone, King Taeho interrogated him. He desired to make the truth known. But the cruel king stood silent with his head hung low.

King Yaswant was irritated by his silence and asked, "Where has your valour gone? I have a strong suspicion that someone may have assisted in your attack on Taeho. Come on, tell me who it is?"

"Nobody helped me; it was just me," the ruthless king abruptly said.

Prince Tejas, "Are you sure about that? Then how were you able to track the entire route of the journey? Don't try to fool us. Speak up."

"Oh dear, I do not think he would speak a word," Rani Nanda said as she stepped forward. "He is loyal to his master. Maybe Lim Maya could help us with that, right?"

The whole crowd and King Taeho were shocked to hear that.

What could she possibly say about the attack?

Lim Maya started to sweat badly and said, "What..what could I tell you about that?"

King Yaswant replied in anger, "There you go, the master of acting; do you think that you could hide the truth forever? You are wrong. Now speak up. Why would you try to kill your son?"

Lim Maya's expression changed, and she retorted, "My son? Never. He is only my stepson. I never loved him."

"He may be your stepson, but how could you murder your own son, Prince Lim Jae Wook?" Rani Nanda retorted. "Say something, you monster."

Lim Maya started to panic. Suddenly, two maids caught her while she planned to run away.

"You have been caught red-handed this time." Prince Tejas said as he walked up to her. "Now speak, woman."

After learning the harsh truth, Taeho was in a trembling state.

He loved her as his mother; how could she kill her son, his beloved brother? Without being able to speak, he just stood there. Lim Maya was trying hard to free herself.

"Still, you do not have any proof that I killed my son; you need to prove my crime, and then you can punish me," she yelled.

"Who said we do not have any proof with us?" asked King Yaswant. "Son, bring them in."

Prince Tejas went to bring them in.

An old man and a young girl walked in. King Yaswant asked them to introduce themselves to the king.

"Your Majesty, I am Min Seok; I am an artist, and this is my daughter, Eun Sook," the elderly man said. "I had one more daughter, and she is no longer alive. Her name was Hye Min. Your brother was in love with her. Both of them were killed on their way to the palace. Your mother killed them."

"What?" Taeho cried out.

"Yes, your majesty, your mother killed them," the old man continued. "I happened to learn about it from my daughter. She will tell you the rest."

The elderly man began to sob loudly because he was unable to speak. How can a father talk about the death of his beloved daughter, whom he loved and lived for? The father was unlucky to see her lifeless body, which was once full of life and joy. The face that brought him peace and happiness has now vanished into the darkness. The first voice to call him father...

"Your majesty," said Eun Sook. "I will tell you the truth. That day, when Prince Lim Jae Wook came to invite my sister to the palace for the coronation ceremony, they went to speak in private. I eavesdropped because I was curious about what they were saying. I overheard them talking about Lim Maya, plotting to assassinate you prior to your coronation."

"Tell me everything that happened; I want to know," declared Taeho. She continued.

"While he was coming to our house, he saw his mother along with a few men having a secret discussion near the borders. He went near them and listened to what they were saying. When he found out she intended to kill you, he was shocked. She was planning it with your father's enemy. He wanted to take revenge. You have now caught the same man. Without anyone noticing, Prince Lim Jae Wook left the area. Your brother was explaining the whole thing to my sister. While I was listening to them, I unknowingly caught their attention. I was asked not to share it with anyone else. He promised me he would let you know about it. Both of them left our place to reach the palace. But... later, they were found dead. I felt disturbed. I told my father about the things that they said, and he wanted the world to know the truth. We learned that King Yaswant would be attending the event. My father only trusted him. We went to meet him on his way to the province. We told him everything we knew. He assured me that my sister would receive justice. He also asked us not to reveal this to anyone because sometimes our lives could also be in danger."

Taeho angrily turned to Lim Maya and said, "Mother, why would you do this to me? What exactly did I do to offend you? I only loved you."

She retorted with contempt, "Love, huh? Who wants your love? Hear me out—this was not the first time. I would kill anybody who came in between to mess with me. Your mother, your father, my son, his father, and that girl who was in love with my son."

CHAPTER SIXTEEN

Upon hearing of her abrupt revelation, everyone was stunned.

She spoke as if she had won. "What, don't you believe? Let me tell you the stories you never knew. Your father—I loved him and wanted to become the queen of the province with all its riches and might. So then my palace sent a proposal to the province. But your father had already fallen in love with your mother. If I couldn't have your father, then nobody should. This was something I had planned for years. To convince others that I had changed my mind, I married another man. Lim Jae Wook's father was a fool who loved me, not knowing that I would kill him. Even the birth of Lim Jae Wook was part of my strategy to convince everybody that I was happy with my family. I poisoned him and became a widow."

Taeho's eyes started to well up. Prince Tejas saw this and came near to comfort him.

Rani Nanda asked out of her anger, "Now tell me, woman, did you have any involvement in killing my sister Hye-Jung?"

"Well, I killed her. If she were still alive, she would rule as the queen and I hated that. I once made a friendly visit when she was pregnant with Taeho. I offered her some exotic fruits, which contained slow-acting poison and left no trace of it. She died because of bleeding; it was the effect of that poison. I intended to kill the baby also, but even today I don't know how he survived."

Rani Nanda rushed over to attack the woman, but Prince Tejas stopped her.

"I killed everybody. And his father disagreed with making me queen of the province, and I killed him too. And about my son, that brat overheard my conversation with his enemy. I saw him in the woods but pretended not to notice. We caught him and his ladylove on their way back. He disagreed with becoming king and loved a girl from the lower class. I warned him not to disclose. But he was blinded by sibling love. I killed him and that girl with my own hands. Nobody ever knew about this. I teamed up with your father's enemy to kill you and become the mighty queen. But I never knew about this old man and his dumb daughter. If I did, I would've already killed them."

The whole crowd started to gasp in wonder about how a woman could become so cruel

Taeho abruptly yelled, "Enough of you. How dare you kill them all? You could have killed me instead. I would have happily offered it to you. You deserve no mercy."

"I would have also killed you. That one time, you were saved from the sudden attack. He escaped, and I know nothing about that idiot now. I leaked the route information. But I missed this time." Lim Maya replied

King Yaswant suddenly asked, "Who said that? We already caught him while he was trying to escape. He already confessed that both of you and the cruel king were behind all this. And there is more to know. When Min-Seok told us about the sinful deeds of Lim Maya, we planned a secret mission. We knew that evidence was required to prove her wrong. We couldn't trust anybody from your place to assign it. It was only because I was afraid of what would occur if they betrayed me and hurt you. So I appointed my trusted person to take up the task. The chief commander of my province's army was disguised as a commoner. The chief was a member of the group who remained in the territory. The chief was compiling all the evidence related to Lim Maya's wrongdoings. You have always been protected from numerous attacks by my commander-in-chief. Even today, you are saved."

King Taeho was astounded by what he had heard.

The crowd started to chant, demanding that the real saviour be revealed.

King Yaswant silenced the crowd.

"People, I understand your emotions. I could only say how much risk my chief had taken to save your king. Before that, tell us what we need to do with these sinners?"

They were to be put to death, per King Taeho's directive. "We will kill them, we will kill them," the crowd chanted.

The mob became furious and was ready to attack the culprits. King Taeho requested to reveal who the mystery saviour was, as he was eagerly waiting to share his gratitude.

"To King Taeho and the people of the province, let me introduce the chief commander of the army of the Praudapuri state, Princess Tejaswini," King Yaswant said with pride.

Shocking, shocking, shocking
A princess disguised as an ordinary person.

A woman covering her face started to come forward from the crowd. People began to applaud for the princess. They could not wait to see her face. The princess walked steadily towards the royal family. She greeted them as she stood in front of them.

"Greetings, Maharaj and Maharani."

"Greetings dear daughter."

What their daughter!
Shocking, shocking, shocking

People were aware that the king and queen had a daughter. However, they never saw the daughter.

"Dear child, now introduce yourself and greet the king of the province."

She obeyed and stood in front of Taeho. He was speechless and became eager to see the face of his Saviour.

She slowly removed the cloth that had been covering her face.

"Greetings, King Taeho. I am Princess Tejaswini, the daughter of King Yaswant and Rani Nanda, and the chief commander of Praudapuri's army," she greeted him.

Shock shock shock

What? Padma, was the princess in disguise?

The entire audience, including the king, was speechless. The day had already been full of surprises and revelations. But they had not anticipated such a stunning turn of events.

"Padma!..." said the king, puzzled.

"That is what we affectionately call her," Prince Tejas responded.

"My queen offered me lotuses of love, so we named our daughter Padma; it means lotus." King Yaswant added

The picture is clear now. Princess Tejaswini was assigned to protect the king while disguised as Padma. Lim Maya went insane after discovering Padma's true identity. None of them expected a twist in the story. Lim Maya was caught off guard.

Taeho was brought back to his senses when Prince Tejas suddenly called him. He ordered Lim Maya and her associates to be released into the crowd and punished according to their wishes. The sinners became traumatised. They were beaten, stabbed, and eventually killed by the mob. The guards removed the dead bodies and buried them. Finally, justice was restored.

The audience began to applaud for Princess Tejaswni. To them, she was Padma, a commoner who lived with them.

"Dear brothers and sisters, I only did my duty, which was assigned to me," Princess Tejaswini said to the crowd.

She continued, "I kept my promise to my father. I made sure that King Taeho was not attacked by the evil Lim Maya. And I would always be the Padma you all knew and loved. Long live justice."

The crowd applauded for her.

She turned to the king and said, "Your majesty, I apologise for faking my identity. It was all I could do. I am sorry." She then went near her parents, and they embraced each other.

Taeho's mind was racing with joy. The woman he adored was also his saviour. She is his destiny. He was so happy in the end that he started crying. He pondered how brave she would have to be to pose as an ordinary person in order to save his life.

He had only seen her when she was a kid. She spent all her time in her grandfather's province.

Everything was settled now; many hours had already passed after the commotion.

New dawn after the cruel dusk

CHAPTER SEVENTEEN

The province celebrated the spring festival. This time, all curses have been lifted, and happiness has returned to everyone. The ceremonies were successful. King Yaswant and Rani Nanda were finally relieved because they could see how happy King Taeho was after all those events. He has gone through a lot at such a young age. They are getting ready to return to India after the ceremonies are over. The love and attention they have shown to King Taeho made him extremely happy and grateful. They send their daughter to his rescue. The enemies would have suspected the secret plan if it were Prince Tejas in place of Padma because he was already known to everybody there. The Indian family came to bid their farewells. They hugged each other and wished to meet him soon.

Princess Tejaswini maintained a serious stance throughout. She is the commander-in-chief. She was in her official attire. Her face displayed the elegance she possessed. He now understood the significance of her short hair. She might become uncomfortable during the swordplay. But when Prince Tejas saw her at his palace, why did he inquire about it? Maybe to persuade their adversaries that they were not related. It might be a part of the play. Everyone did a good job of playing their parts and left no traces.

It was all for him.

He talked with the king and queen. Prince Tejas asked for an apology as the siblings pretended that they never knew each other.

To that, Taeho replied, "I can understand that. I am forever grateful to you, my friend." They hugged each other.

He then walked over to Princess Tejaswini and said, "Thank you for everything that you've done for me. No words could ever convey my gratitude to you. And I hope you will remember us."

"Your majesty. I completed my mission. Now I may go back to my home. Thank you." She replied without any sort of emotion. She mounted her horse and started riding without replying to the king's proposal.

He knows her very well, maybe more than he knows about himself. It was as if she were a part of him. She loves him. She's pretending that she has no interest. But he is happy now. Her parents would be very happy when they learned about his love for their daughter.

He loved her before he knew who she was, and he still does. Love hasn't changed.

He would love to worship her like a goddess. She is one of a kind. The Indian royals went back to their country. Now that many more months have passed, everything is going well and happily. King Taeho was unable to stop thinking about his Padma, the woman he worships and who he has an unwavering love for. He decided that he would pay a visit to King Yaswant's province. He was preparing for the trip. A messenger came to him and conveyed that Prince Tejas had arrived to meet him.

CHAPTER EIGHTEEN

His brother...

He became happy and went to welcome him. Both friends met after a long time. Prince Tejas has now arrived to invite his friend to his marriage. He is going to get married to the woman he loves, the princess he mentioned earlier. Taeho was happy to hear that. He considered discussing his love as well. Prince Tejas felt that he had something to say and asked, "Is there anything that you want to tell me? What is it?"

Taeho was hesitant at first, but later he thought to speak up.

"It is about Padma, I mean Princess Tejaswini," he said, then continued to tell the whole story. With a smile on his face, Prince Tejas carefully listened to him. He could tell how passionate he was by the look in his eyes. Prince Tejas was happy to hear that.

"I loved her as Padma, but when I came to know about her, not only did I love her even more, but I also respected her. I hope your parents will be happy about this relationship."

"Definitely! In fact, they would agree to this marriage. Our father would be the happiest. Padma is our gem. She is a talented warrior who received her training from our grandfather. She possesses unique abilities, and I am actively attempting to learn new things from her."

He started to sing the praises of his beloved sister—about her wit, goodness, and other qualities. King Taeho was determined that she was a pure soul. Prince Tejas then departed after inviting the king to his wedding. He also promised to talk to his parents about this issue. He was confident that this would mark the start of his happy family life. King Taeho travelled to India a few weeks later to attend his friend's wedding. His joy was beyond his ability to control. He saw Princess Tejaswini in her traditional attire. A woman full of grace and elegance, reflecting ethnic Indian beauty. He couldn't take his eyes off her. He was mesmerised by how she carried herself. He went to greet the king and queen.

They knew about his love for Padma and were happy to have him as their son-in-law. Princess Tejaswini appeared to be tough while engaging with Taeho. She pretended that she was uninterested in initiating a conversation with him. The family found her behaviour strange. Padma and other dancers performed a traditional dance style as part of the wedding ceremony. Taeho was immersed in her performance. He liked the music, which was played with a variety of instruments. He overheard the princes of other provinces complimenting her while she performed.

"Look at her, how graceful she is!"

"She is a trained dancer."

"No doubt she is the smartest among all other princesses."

"She is intelligent."

"I heard that she learned it from her mother."

"She would make an excellent queen."

"She won the debate with the scholars from the East."

"I wish I could marry her."

He was both pleased and envious when he heard them. He was happy to hear good things about his queen. But what if she agrees to marry someone else? No, she won't ever do that, he believed. Her heart belongs to him.

There was something divine about her, something he couldn't explain. He suddenly turned to look at the newlyweds and wondered what it would be like if it were him and Padma. He blushed thinking about it. The king and queen joined the dance, and they invited Taeho to join them. They all danced to the drum beats. It felt like HOME. They celebrated the moment to the fullest.

The marriage ceremony went well, and he gave the newlywed couple a lot of gifts from Korea. He also invited them to visit Korea. Taeho agreed to stay with them for a week as their special guest after Rani

Nanda insisted on it. The next morning, when we woke up, he went out to search for Padma. He asked one of the guards whom he saw on his way. The guard replied that she must be on the practise ground. He went over to the practise field. He observed Princess Tejaswini teaching martial arts to a group of young children. What a passionate and thoughtful lady! He approached them slowly. She chose not to turn around, even though she was aware of his presence. The children identified him and greeted him.

Princess Tejaswini turned around to greet him. She was hesitant to look into his eyes. He invited her for a friendly match.

"Princess Tejaswini, shall I invite you for a match? I heard that you were the only princess who excelled in swordplay."

"I make no claims to being a master of swords, Your Majesty."

"Why? However, it was you who acted with courage to save the king of the province."

The children who gathered there didn't know about that incident. They all gasped upon hearing that. They were equally proud and happy for their princess.

When the kids heard that, they got excited. They started to cheer for them. The princess couldn't disagree. They took up the stick fight. He was stunned by her moves. Prince Tejas was right; she has great skills. He was losing the battle, but she gave up, leading him to win the match.

"Your Majesty, you win."

"No Padma, you made me win. Why would you do that? Even if I failed in front of you, I would not feel ashamed. Because (you are my life) you are my saviour."

In order to express his gratitude, he got down on one knee and said, "I will always be grateful."

She was shocked to see him bow down in front of her. It was not so common for a man to kneel in front of a woman. She left there after dismissing the session for her students. The kids surrounded the king and started cheering him on.

"Did she fail the match?" asked a child from the group.

"No, she won my heart," Taeho said in his head.

"Will you bring her with you when you go back to your place, dear king?" asked one of the children.

"She is a woman with her own choices. She can make her own decisions." Taeho replied with a proud smile on his face and lowered himself to the child's height.

"Even if I do not do that, your princess will eventually become my queen."

"Oh! So our Princess will become a queen?"

The kids could not contain their joy, so they started singing happy songs. Taeho felt delighted to see the children happy for their princess.

After spending some time with the children, he left to search for her. But she was nowhere to be seen. He was invited to take part in the royal family's breakfast. He reached the dining hall and saw Princess Tejaswini already sitting in her place. He sat next to her since there was a vacant seat. Tejaswini silently ate her meal while others were busy chit-chatting while taking their bites. She seemed devoid of feeling. Rani Nanda suggested that the newlywed couple, along with King Taeho and Princess Nanda, visit her native province. They all agreed to that. Princess Tejaswini was happy that she would be able to meet her grandfather.

She finished her meal and left the hall before everyone else. This gave room for the rest of the members to have a discussion. They had already heard from Prince Tejas about King Taeho's desire to wed Princess Tejaswini. Rani Nanda said that they are really happy. Their daughter has complete discretion in her decision.

King Yaswant said, "Son, we will never force her to take a decision. Everything is up to her choice."

"Don't worry brother, I know she loves you; otherwise, why would she risk her life to save yours?" replied Prince Tejas. Taeho explained that he feels like she is ignoring her feelings for him. Princess Indu, the spouse of Prince Tejas, speculated that she might be ignoring him because of something bothering her. They anticipate that this trip will remove all the obstacles. He was delighted to see the entire family express hope and support for his love.

Why not? In the end, it's for Padma and Taeho.

CHAPTER NINETEEN

The four of them travelled to Ananyapuri two days later. They were all delighted to see the king. The old king gave them a hearty welcome. They enjoyed themselves there. Prince Tejas talked about Taeho's love interest. The king promised that he would help him with it. He insisted they talk to each other. Padma had no idea about these. For that, Princess Tejaswini was assigned to take Taeho to show him around the kingdom. She couldn't disagree with her grandfather. She escorted him on the trip. Only the two of them. She took him to every possible place so that he would be able to enjoy the land's beauty. He was happy to see that they were being greeted by people as they travelled.

So many of them presented food and flowers. They were surprised to see the Korean king speaking their language. He had a sense of belonging. He watched in awe as Princess Tejaswini addressed each of them by their names or respectful titles. She was personally acquainted with each of them. It is not easy to remember every one of them. Once again, she earned his respect. He could not help but admire her. They walked for many hours and reached the farmland.

It was harvest season. The trees were filled with fruits. People working in the field and kids having fun. They sang folk songs while working in the field. The enthralling sight of blooming flowers. He felt that the time was right to bring up the subject. He started the conversation.

"So what should I call you, Padma or Tejaswini?"

"You may call whatever you wish your majesty."

"What if I call you the future queen of the state?"

"Then I would respectfully object."

"Why, why Padma? Can't you see the love I hold for you? I loved you even before I knew that you were a princess. I loved you as a person. I love your soul."

"I know your passionate love for me. But I am afraid. What if I won't be able to love you the way you do? Why add more trouble? You already have gone through a lot, and I do not wish to add more to your agony."

"My beloved, there you go; that's what love is. You care for me; for my well-being. What else could I ask for? I assure you that you haven't added any trouble to my life yet, and I believe you won't ever do that to me. I am confident in you. Your love is unique, and I would treasure that for my whole life. I was afraid that perhaps you didn't find me find better choice-"

"No. never, please, do not say anything like that, you were the best person. It was all because of my overthinking that I thought of distancing myself from you. Back then, I believed that if I spent all of my time with you, I would not be able to find the enemy. But even at that distance, I was suffering. I loved you from afar. I would offer my life to protect you."

"You already did. *No love is greater than sacrificing one's own life for the ones you love.* You are not inferior to me, my goddess."

"But what about the cultural differences between us? Will the people be able to accept me as their queen?"

"Why not? My lady, love is what ultimately brings people together. It transcends all differences. They would be delighted to have a loyal queen like you. Imagine the consequences if someone like Lim Maya were to be in charge of the province."

"Then the great province will crumble. I don't want that to happen."

"Neither do I. Consider our fathers. Despite having different cultural backgrounds, they supported one another whenever they needed it. In addition, you, my lady, and my dear brother Tejas and Rani Nanda were there for me. Isn't that the greatest love? I am convinced that you will be my queen, and together we could live a life that even the coming generations would wish for."

The bow to my arrow, the moon to my dreams, the shield to my fears, and the love to my life.

"Neither death nor demons could ever separate us. And our story shall be written with a different ink." She replied.

It was already evening. Twilight.

The skies were purple and blue. They marvelled at the art of the evening sky, with the moon slowly rising from the east-the marble gleam.

She said, "Let the purple and blue of the twilight sky remain as the seal of our love—the *MIZPAH*."

From Dusk to Dawn.

THE END.

About the Author

A human who takes comfort from everything that could add life to self -writes stories with a different ink and cherishes life's essence.